The Witch's Big Toe

Illustrated by Eileen Browne

Wendy is a thoroughly modern witch – she even drives a petrol-filled broomstick – but when it comes to being a *successful* witch, which means do at least one bad turn to someone every day, Wendy finds her magic often leaves her the worst off!

RALPH WRIGHT

The Witch's Big Toe

MAMMOTH

First published 1983 by Methuen Children's Books Ltd
Magnet paperback edition published 1985
Reprinted 1985, 1987
Reissued 1989 by Mammoth,
an imprint of Mandarin Paperbacks
Michelin House, 81 Fulham Road, London SW3 6RB
Reprinted 1990

Mandarin is an imprint of the Octopus Publishing Group

Text copyright © 1983 Ralph Wright
Illustrations copyright © 1983 Eileen Browne
Printed and bound in Great Britain
by Cox and Wyman Ltd, Reading

ISBN 0 7497 0166 8

Contents

1   Wendy becomes a witch

Wendy walked along the pavement to school, kicking up the autumn leaves with each step. She was tall and slim, with big dark eyes and an upturned nose which gave her face a cheeky look. Her black hair finished in two wings which hung at each side of her chin.

'Boring old school!' she muttered.

Usually Wendy went everywhere in a great hurry, but today she wasn't in the mood. She got slower and slower. Then she had an idea that cheered her up.

'I wish I could put magic spells on everyone to make them do funny things! That would make life more interesting.'

Wendy's face brightened at this thought. 'I suppose I would have to be a witch to do that,' she said. 'What a lot of fun I'd have!

That Miss Crumb who tells me off for not sitting still – I'd put a spell on her to make her itch all over, then *she* wouldn't be able to sit still either! And that girl, Clarissa, who puts her tongue out at me – I'd put a spell on her so she couldn't get her tongue back in again. What a funny sight that would be!' Wendy giggled.

The idea of being a witch cheered Wendy up so much that she skipped cheerfully along to school with more like her usual energy.

But she was feeling glum again by the time she turned in the school gates.

'I don't suppose I ever will be a witch,' she thought, 'and it will be another boring old day at school.'

There was no-one in the playground.

'That's funny!' thought Wendy 'I must be late.'

She rushed in the doors. There was something strange about the entrance hall too. Where were the children's paintings that should have been on the wall? Where was the aquarium full of goldfish by the headmaster's door? And there were cobwebs and spiders everywhere! Whenever Wendy moved, spiders' webs tickled her neck.

The strange thing was, there were lots of broomsticks about. They were the old-fashioned sort, made of bundles of sticks.

'Funny!' said Wendy. 'All these broomsticks, but nobody's cleaned the cobwebs away!'

Wendy was so busy looking up at the cobwebs, that she tripped over another broomstick lying on the floor.

'Ouch!' said Wendy, who had fallen flat on her face. Then she heard a cackle of laughter.

She looked up to see the strange figure of an old, old woman in a long blue gown. She had long bony fingers and a pointed nose with a hairy spot on it. She wore a tall hat on her head.

'It can't be,' thought Wendy, 'but she looks just like a witch!'

'Hello, Wendy,' croaked the old woman. 'So you want to be a witch?'

'Yes, but how did you know?' Wendy asked.

'By magic, of course! What's the use of being a witch if you haven't got magic?'

'So you *are* a witch!' said Wendy, thrilled.

'I'm the Blue Witch,' said the old woman, 'and if you want to be a witch too, you'd better hurry along to your lessons. You won't get your Witch Certificate by missing your lessons, you know.'

'Yes, Miss! I mean, Blue Witch! Thanks!'

Wendy rushed off in such excitement that she tripped over another broomstick and fell flat on her face again!

Before she could get up a black cat came and licked her nose.

'Hello!' said Wendy, who was very fond of animals. 'You're as black as night. I shall call you Midnight!' And from then on Midnight followed Wendy about wherever she went.

At last Wendy got to the classroom and sat at a desk. Midnight went to sleep at her feet. In front of the class was a wizard, with a tall hat and a long grey robe with stars all over it. There was no sign of Miss Crumb – or any of her friends. The class was full though. There were some girls her own age and lots of grown ups, even some very old ladies. It really had turned into a Witch's school!

'Listen carefully!' said the Grey Wizard,

and all the pupils sat up straight. 'Here is the first rule.'

He waved his pointed stick towards the blackboard behind him, and some words magically appeared:

I MUST DO A GOOD TURN TO SOMEBODY EVERY DAY.

'Oh, sorry!' said the Grey Wizard sheepishly, 'I'm a Scoutmaster in the evenings, you see.'

And he rubbed out the word 'good' using the sleeve of his robe and wrote in another word so that it now read, I MUST DO A **BAD** TURN TO SOMEBODY EVERY DAY.

'Follow that rule and you will be a good witch.'

Wendy wrote it down carefully.

'Now, I see you have not come in the proper uniform,' continued the Grey Wizard. 'We'll soon change that.'

He waved his stick again – Wendy realized it was a magic wand – and suddenly all his pupils were dressed in long gowns of different colours, and pointed hats.

'Now you all look like witches!' beamed the Grey Wizard, as Wendy and the others admired their new clothes.

'Back to work! Today's lesson is How to Cast Magic Spells. Rule number one: Spells work best in nasty weather: thunder, lightning, snowstorms, rainstorms, hailstorms, wind – these are best of all. Rule number two: only spells that rhyme will work properly. Like this!' And he said:

> *'Give my magic wand a shake*
> *And it will turn into a snake!'*

And sure enough, there was a fine green and yellow snake, which hissed a bit, then slith-
ered off under the door.

'Now one of *you* try,' said the Grey Wizard, and Wendy jumped

12

when she saw he was pointing at her. Then she heard the cat purring at her feet and had an idea. And she said:

'This little cat, that I called Midnight,
Will change to a lion, and give you a fright!'

The cat seemed to have gone, and Wendy thought her spell hadn't worked. But suddenly the Grey Wizard bolted out of the room, followed by all his pupils, shrieking and squealing and tumbling over each other in their hurry to escape.

'What on earth has come over them all?' puzzled Wendy. Then an enormous roar behind her made her jump two feet in the air, and she turned to see a huge lion, looking extremely fierce.

Wendy was out of the school in a flash, and didn't stop running until she got home.

'Oh dear!' wailed Wendy, as she tumbled into bed. 'I did want to do everything right, but I seem to have caused a lot of trouble! Tomorrow I'll try and do better.'

The next day, Wendy rushed to get to the classroom first, determined to do everything right. On her way in she felt something stroke her ankle. It was the cat.

'Hello, Midnight!' called Wendy in delight.

'I like you much better as a cat than a lion. I'm glad the magic has worn off.'

This time another wizard, quite small and dressed in a green gown, stood in front of the class. He had a long, straggly beard.

'Bad morning to you all!' he said cheerfully.

'Bad morning to you too, sir!' his pupils replied eagerly.

'Today's lesson will be on the care and control of black cats,' said the Green Wizard.

Wendy, stroking Midnight who was curled up on her knee, looked round and noticed for the first time that all the other pupils had a black cat with them too!

'Every witch must have a black cat,' the Green Wizard went on. 'You must feed your cat on ...' his voice faded away and his pupils were amazed to see the wizard growing fainter and then disappearing from sight altogether.

A few looked around the room to try to find the wizard. One looked in a cupboard and out fell a skeleton on top of her! It couldn't be the Green Wizard; it was much too tall. Some said they should all go home, but just then the Green Wizard began to appear again, still talking '. . . I hope you will all remember that; it is very important.'

14

'But sir!' said Wendy, 'we didn't hear it because you disappeared!'

'Oh really?' smiled the Green Wizard. 'Yes, I *do* keep disappearing, don't I? I mixed some very powerful vanishing powder last week and spilt some in my pockets. I've been vanishing now and again ever since. Never mind. The next thing about black cats is how to train them. Every morning you must ...'

But no-one heard what they had to do as the Green Wizard had disappeared again. And the same thing happened all day; every time he started to tell them something interesting he vanished, and when he *was* there he never got round to telling them what he was going to say.

'Oh dear!' wailed Wendy as she walked home, with Midnight skipping along ahead of her. 'I shall never learn witchcraft and get my Witch's Certificate at this rate. I hope tomorrow will be better!'

The next day the Blue Witch was waiting to take the class.

'After today's lesson,' the Blue Witch began, in the croaky voice that made Wendy rather scared, 'you will not need to ride on buses or in cars like other people. You will be able to ride your very own broomstick.'

15

She snapped her fingers and mumbled a spell, and Wendy was thrilled to see a cupboard door open and a flock of broomsticks fly out. A broomstick landed in front of each pupil.

Wendy gingerly picked up her broomstick, afraid it might fly off again on its own, and followed the Blue Witch outside with the others on to the college lawn.

'We are not quite ready,' said the Blue Witch, and snapped her fingers. Instantly every pupil witch had an L-plate on her back to show she was a learner. 'Now get on your broomsticks!'

Wendy leapt astride hers, but the broomstick had other ideas. It reared up like a nervous horse, tipping Wendy on her back with her legs in the air!

'Try again, Wendy,' the Witch said kindly, 'and this time give it a stroke and say something nice to it.'

'All right,' replied Wendy doubtfully. 'What a *good* little broomstick you are! Keep still now, you clever little broomstick! I'm sure we shall be good friends!' Warily she got on the broomstick again, and this time it didn't seem to mind.

By now everyone else was swooping and

dipping around the lawn a few feet off the ground. So Wendy thought, 'Here goes!' and shut her eyes tightly before calling, 'Up, broomstick!'

It shot up in the air, passing all the others, and didn't stop till it reached the school roof. Wendy was terrified.

'Help!' she wailed. 'I can't stand heights!'

'Come down at once, Wendy!' called the Blue Witch.

Wendy clung to the broomstick and whispered, 'Down, broomstick!' It leaped off the roof; Wendy lost her balance but hung on upside down, as the broomstick swooped back to the lawn – and knocked the Blue Witch off her feet!

'I'm so sorry!' said Wendy, as she helped the Blue Witch up again. 'I don't think I'll ever get the hang of this. I'm much too embarrassed to stay here. I wish I could just disappear!'

By accident, Wendy had said this in rhyme. And so of course the spell worked! There was a flash and Wendy did disappear, and the next thing she knew the broomstick, Midnight the cat, and Wendy arrived all in a heap in her bedroom at home.

In the morning Wendy didn't want to go

to school. 'I've made an awful mess of it,' she told Midnight. 'I'm sure I won't get my Certificate. The cat mewed sadly. 'But I must go,' she realised with alarm. 'I'll have to take the broomstick back.'

So Wendy set off on her broomstick. 'You must go slowly and carefully today,' she told it, 'and not more than ankle-high off the ground.'

Perhaps the broomstick was ashamed of yesterday's antics, for it behaved beautifully, and Wendy flew slowly to the school, stopping at traffic lights, signalling carefully to turn corners, and waiting at zebra crossings for surprised people to cross the road.

The Blue Witch, and the Green Wizard were already at the school, and the Grey Wizard soon arrived. They were giving out the Witch's Certificates to those who had passed.

'Ah, Wendy!' said the Blue Witch. 'Here is your certificate. Well done! You've passed.'

Wendy was amazed. 'But I got everything wrong!'

'Nonsense! Your disappearing spell worked very well yesterday, didn't it? So you got full marks for Casting Spells. And your Broomstick Driving was excellent this morning. The

19

Grey Wizard followed you all the way to school and gave you full marks. As for Care and Control of Black Cats – I have never seen a happier cat than yours!'

Midnight purred proudly. Wendy beamed with pleasure and took her Certificate.

'Now I'm a real witch!' said Wendy proudly. 'What an exciting life I shall have!'

And she did.

2 · Things get on top of Wendy

The day after Wendy got her Witch's Certificate, she rushed out of the house in great high spirits and flew up the road on her broomstick.

'Now to try out my new powers of witchcraft!' she said.

Suddenly she remembered something.

'Stop, Broomstick!' she called. 'I forgot to take off my L-plate. Now I've passed my Broomstick Driving Test I don't have to wear it any more.' She felt very proud.

Wendy reached behind her, but couldn't manage to get the L-plate off the back of her gown.

'What shall I do?' she wondered in dismay.

'Miaow!' said a small voice. It was Midnight. Wendy had left home in such a rush that the cat had been left behind. Midnight leaped on Wendy's shoulder. Then she dived down Wendy's back and hung there by her back claws, which were firmly stuck in the shoulder of Wendy's gown. With her front paws, Midnight managed to pull loose the sticky corners of the L-plate.

'Oh, thank you, Midnight!' Wendy said in relief. 'I can see you're going to be a very useful witch's cat. Come and ride in front of me.'

So Midnight perched on the front end of the broomstick's handle and they all set off, Midnight purring happily.

But the front end of the broomstick was now too heavy. It pointed down too much and Wendy kept coming to land before she wanted to.

'You'll have to come and sit at the back, Midnight. Here, where all the twigs are.'

So Midnight sat on the back end of the broomstick. But now the front end pointed up too much. Wendy kept soaring high in the air, and at last she got stuck in the top of an oak tree in the park.

'This won't do at all, Midnight,' Wendy decided. 'You'll have to sit on my shoulder to keep the broomstick properly balanced.'

So from then on, whenever they went flying, Midnight always perched on Wendy's shoulder.

From the top of the oak tree, Wendy saw

some children in the playground. She eagerly swooped down to show off her new broomstick. They watched admiringly from the swings and climbing frames. All but James. James sat at the bottom of the slide and jeered at Wendy.

'Look at that silly hat she's got on! I'll soon knock it off her head!' And he started throwing stones at Wendy's hat.

'Right!' said Wendy, getting cross. 'I'll teach you not to throw stones.'

She said:

> *'It'll make you gasp and grunt,*
> *When that slide works back to front!'*

A look of dismay came over James's face as he suddenly lost his balance at the end of the slide. Then he began to move – upwards! He slid faster and faster until at the top he shot into the air, shrieking. His arms and legs waved wildly in all directions.

He flew through the air and landed with a splash in the paddling pool.

Wendy laughed and laughed as James ran off, soaking wet. She did enjoy being able to play tricks on people! She was so busy laughing she didn't see P.C. Trunch, the portly local policeman, stroll up to the slide. He liked making friends and chatting with the children on his patch.

'Oh no!' wailed Wendy. 'Don't sit there!'

It was too late. P.C. Trunch sat on the end of the slide.

'I'm off!' said Wendy. 'Up, broomstick!'

The surprised constable slid feet first up the

slide and shot into the air. In mid-air he crashed – right into Wendy's broomstick! Both fell to the ground with a thump!

It was some time before Wendy got her breath back.

'It's not as much fun being a witch as I thought!' she gasped.

P.C. Trunch staggered off. He looked dazed and walked in zig-zags, scratching his head and muttering, 'They'll never believe this down at the station!'

Wendy flew home to rub some ointment into her sore back.

'I didn't know witchcraft would turn out to be so painful, Midnight,' she said ruefully, as she fed the cat. 'Never mind, I'm sure I'll get the hang of it tomorrow.'

The next day, Wendy Witch set off to the shopping precinct. She was a little stiff, so she had not rushed far down the street this time before Midnight caught up with her and leapt on her shoulder.

'Come on broomstick! Let's fly high today!'

Wendy's high spirits were back. What a thrill it was to be a witch! She felt sorry for the people down below who had to ride on buses or in cars while she could soar above the trees. She had quite got over her fear of

25

heights. And with her magic she could do anything she wanted!

Wendy told her broomstick to glide down into the precinct. The broomstick flew a couple of turns around the fountain then came to rest. Wendy propped it up against the wall outside the supermarket and went in with Midnight.

But Wendy couldn't find any of the things she wanted on the shelves, so she took her shopping list to the counter to ask the shop keeper.

'Have you got any bat's wool, please, Mr. Price?' Wendy asked timidly. 'I couldn't see any toe of frog on the shelves either.'

The tall shop keeper glared fiercely down at Wendy from beneath his bushy eyebrows. 'Any what, young lady? Are you trying to make a fool of me?'

'Of course not, Mr. Price!' she assured him. 'But now I'm a witch I shall need these ingredients to make magic potions.'

'A witch!' snorted Mr. Price. 'You children, always coming in here wasting my time with your silly tales. Go on, be off with you, I'm a busy man!'

Just then, Midnight jumped on the counter. She had seen some sugar mice and wanted to chase them.

'And take your cat out of here!' roared Mr. Price, sweeping Midnight off the counter with a blow of his arm.

Midnight gave a frightened 'miaow' and Wendy sprang to help her. She knew you shouldn't take animals into a food shop, but she was afraid the little black cat had hurt her leg.

Glaring at Mr. Price, she said:

'Bad-tempered Mr. Price, now you
Can suffer with a bad leg too!'

A strange thing happened. Mr. Price, who had gone to the back of the shop to fetch some big boxes, was amazed to feel his right leg begin to grow. Soon it was quite a bit longer than his left leg. This gave him a very comical look as he tilted over to one side. With his pile of big boxes he tottered down the shop, swaying alarmingly from side to side.

Wendy laughed and laughed.

But as he reached the counter, Mr. Price lost his balance, and the pile of boxes, full of heavy tins of food, came tumbling down – right on top of Wendy Witch!

This time it was even longer before Wendy got her breath back. Even then she could

hardly move under all those boxes. Mr. Price and some other customers lifted the boxes off.

'I *am* sorry, my dear,' he said. 'Are you all right? I wish I hadn't told you off. I can't think why I fell over. I think there's something the matter with my leg.'

Wendy hastily muttered a spell under her breath to put Mr. Price's leg right again. Then she thanked him and the customers for their help.

'I'm quite all right now,' she told them, and hobbled out of the shop.

She climbed stiffly back on the broomstick and flew off home to put more ointment on her sore back.

'I'm black and blue all over!' she moaned to Midnight, as she gave her a big saucer of milk. 'Every time I put a nasty spell on someone, I seem to get the worst of it myself!'

The next day, Wendy could hardly walk out of the house, she was so stiff, and Midnight caught up with her before she had closed the front door. But Wendy's high spirits were soon back again. She was determined to have some fun.

'Come on, Midnight!' she called, climbing stiffly on to her broomstick. 'Let's find someone to play tricks on with my magic!'

Soon they saw an ice-cream van. Wendy flew down because she knew her friend Jimmy was inside, selling lollipops and ice-cream.

'Morning, Wendy, my love! What will you have today – a Vanilla Glory or a Jimmy's Special?'

A Jimmy's Special had strawberry and lime ice-cream which were just the colours Jimmy liked to dye his hair. As the day was warm, a lot of children were buying ice-creams and, as usual, Jimmy gave the younger ones a bit extra.

Wendy thought he deserved a nice surprise. The van had a big plastic ice-cream cornet on the front of the roof, above the windscreen.

So she said:

> *'Cone, you are not what you seem*
> *From plastic, change to real ice-cream!'*

'Jimmy will get a nice surprise when he finds all that extra ice-cream!' Wendy whispered to Midnight.

All the children had now bought their ice-creams and it was time for Jimmy to move on.

'Goodbye, Wendy!' he called and drove off down the hill. The ice-cream in the huge cone was beginning to melt in the warm sun. Then, a great blob of it slurped down on to the windscreen. Jimmy was driving quite fast and suddenly he couldn't see where he was going. His van began to swerve all over the road, and at the bottom of the hill was the shopping precinct!

Jimmy would drive straight into it if he couldn't see to turn the corner. And lots of people were shopping there on this nice warm day! Wendy Witch had to think fast.

And she said:

> *'Midnight, go as fast as you can*
> *Turn into a magnet to stop the van!'*

And so it happened. The little cat raced down the hill, sprang into the air, and van-

30

ished in a flash of light. Wendy blinked, and there, before her eyes, a huge horseshoe magnet hung above the road.

The runaway ice-cream van thundered down towards the bottom of the hill. Then the magnet began to pull. The van slowed, and stopped just before the pavement.

Wendy flew down the hill to make sure Jimmy was all right. He got out of the van a bit shakily.

'I don't know how you did that, Wendy,' he said, 'but one thing I'm sure of, you've saved my life by stopping the van. You can have free ice-cream whenever you want after this.'

'At least this time,' Wendy whispered to Midnight, 'nothing fell on top of me!'

But the giant ice-cream, which had been getting sloppier and sloppier in the sun, chose this moment to drop out of its cornet – right on top of Wendy Witch!

3   The witch's big toe

Wendy Witch jumped out of bed with a leap, leaving her blankets in a tangle all over the bedroom. Outside, the sky was black with rain clouds, and she threw the windows open wide, just in time to catch the first big raindrops splashing down.

'What a lovely, awful morning,' she called, all in a thrill. 'It's such a wonderfully rotten morning that I'm bound to be able to do a bad turn to somebody today.'

Full of excitement, Wendy got dressed in no time, in her long black gown and pointed hat. She had three eggs for breakfast – rotten ones of course – and rushed out of the house, just remembering to grab her broomstick from the hall cupboard on the way.

'Bad Morning to you all!' she said cheerfully to the people in the street. But they just looked cross and went on their way. Wendy was a bit upset.

'Was it something I said?' she thought.

Next she saw a milkman driving his float. Wendy squealed to a halt on her broomstick. 'Must remember to get the brakes seen to,' she thought.

'Now's my chance to do a bad turn,' she said, as the milkman picked up a crate of milk.

'Here goes!'

'In his milkman's float he goes
may marbles roll between his toes!'

Suddenly, there were marbles all over the road. The milkman slipped and skidded on the marbles and the crate of milk flew into the air.

Wendy laughed and laughed at the poor milkman sitting in the road, until the crate of milk landed – right on Wendy's big toe!

She hopped up and down the street holding her big toe and shouting 'Ouch' in her loudest voice because her toe hurt so much.

Painfully, she hobbled to her broomstick and flew home to put a bandage on her toe.

'My magic spell wasn't supposed to go like that,' she said. 'Never mind, tomorrow it'll go better.'

The next day, Wendy got out of bed carefully because her toe had swollen to twice its usual size.

Outside it was very windy and Wendy threw open the window just in time to catch a hat that had blown away in the wind.

'What a lovely, horribly windy morning,' she said. It's such a wonderfully rotten day that my bad spell is bound to go well today.'

She was dressed in hardly any time at all, which was a bit slower than yesterday because it was hard to get her tights on over her bad toe. She had three rashers of bacon for breakfast – nice and mouldy of course.

Off she flew down the street calling cheerfully to the people she saw.

'Bad Morning to you all!' But everyone looked away as the broomstick flew past.

'Well really!' thought Wendy. 'You'd think people would be polite enough to answer when I greet them.'

Suddenly her broomstick began to splutter. It was running out of petrol.

'I wish broomsticks would run on magic alone, as they used to,' said Wendy crossly. 'Now I shall have to go to the petrol station.'

She had just got to the garage, carrying her broomstick, when a fat man in a big car rushed past her so fast that she had to jump into a puddle to get out of the way.

The car stopped and the fat man started to

fill up with petrol.

'You should watch where you're walking!' he shouted at Wendy. 'You're a menace on the road!'

'Right!' thought Wendy. 'I shall do you my bad turn for the day.'

And she said:

> *'Fat man who thinks he owns the road,*
> *I'll turn your car into a toad!'*

Just as the man was getting back into his car it became an enormous green toad, as big

as the car had been. He found himself sitting on its back. The giant toad gave a giant croak that scared the fat man so much he nearly fell off. Then the toad started to hop in giant hops round the petrol station.

Wendy was laughing so much that she didn't see what was going to happen.

The toad hopped three times round the petrol pumps. On its last hop it landed – on Wendy's big toe!

Then it hopped away down the street into the distance with the fat man clinging on its back and yelling, 'Help! Help!'

Wendy Witch started hopping too, holding her sore toe. Now it was her turn to hop three times round the petrol pumps, crying 'Oooh! Ouch!' because her toe hurt so much.

By this time the garage man had filled up the broomstick with petrol, so Wendy climbed on and flew home to put another bandage on her big toe.

'My spells don't seem to be working out very well,' she moaned. 'Tomorrow I must try harder.'

The next day Wendy got out of bed very carefully because her toe was swollen to four times its usual size.

She hobbled over to the window and

opened it wide.

'Oh no!' she groaned when she saw the weather. 'What a terrible day for a spell!'

And she was right. It was a lovely, warm sunny day. Not at all the sort of day for a really good spell.

Wendy was dressed in a moment, which was longer than yesterday, because she had to cut a hole in her boot for her bandaged big toe to stick out.

She had sausages for breakfast, with tomatoes that were so old they had gone black and squishy. Then she tried to rush out of the house with her broomstick, but that made her toe hurt. So she hobbled out quite slowly instead.

Down the street, Wendy met a lollipop lady helping the children cross the road to school. They all looked happy because it was such a nice day. Wendy felt bad-tempered because it was an awful day for a spell, and she growled crossly:

> *'Crossing roads gives you no rest,*
> *A pogo-stick will suit you best!'*

The crossing lady's lollipop turned at once into a pogo-stick. It started bouncing about with the lady hanging on in fright. It bounced around the pavement. It bounced across the road and back, and Wendy saw what was going to happen next, but it was too late – it bounced – right on her big toe!

'Ooh-aahh!' wailed Wendy, holding her sore toe.

All this time, the pogo-stick was still bouncing with the lady on top, and the children were shrieking and running about to get out of its way.

Suddenly, one little boy ran out into the road, just as they all heard a car. It was the fat man, driving very fast. His big car had turned back from a toad into a car again.

The little boy was still in the road. He was going to be run over!

Wendy stopped rubbing her toe. And she said:

> '*Little boy in trouble, you*
> *must jump just like a kangaroo!*'

And he leapt high into the air, just as the car zoomed past, and landed safely on the pavement next to Wendy, just missing her poor swollen big toe!

Everyone was very pleased. They all patted Wendy on the back.

'Well done, Wendy!' they said. 'You saved the little boy's life.'

Wendy smiled. 'Sometimes it's nice to do good magic instead of bad,' she thought. 'Perhaps I'd better stick to good magic for a while.' And she rubbed her sore toe. 'At least, until my toe gets better.'

4 · Wendy Witch means well

Wendy Witch had decided to use her magic to do nice things instead of nasty ones.

Excitedly she went to see the witches and wizards she knew to tell them all about her new idea.

'Ridiculous!' said the Grey Wizard. 'Who ever heard of a nice witch?'

'Bad Heavens!' said the small Green Wizard. 'It's your duty as a witch to go round making people miserable!' And he was so indignant that he promptly vanished.

'Well!' croaked the Blue Witch doubtfully, 'I suppose it *might* work. I don't think it's ever been tried before. Do be careful, dear!'

'You're not much help,' sighed Wendy. But she was determined to try her new idea, so she called Midnight, and the two of them flew off on her broomstick to see what nice things they could do.

'Bad Morning – no, *Good* Morning to you all!' she called cheerfully to the people in the street. They all waved back and called, 'Good Morning, Wendy!' Wendy felt a warm glow of niceness already.

She flew down into town, with Midnight on her shoulder. A double-decker bus was travelling along the High Street.

'I'll give the people on the bus a nice surprise!' Wendy told Midnight. And she flew alongside the bus, waving to the people on the top deck.

A white-haired, old lady spotted Wendy first.

'Surely, dear,' she asked her friend, 'that can't really be a witch on a broomstick?'

Her friend shrieked. The passengers on the bus were not used to seeing witches. They all rushed to the windows on one side of the bus. The bus tipped sideways, ran for a while on two wheels along the High Street, and then toppled over on its side with a crash.

'Oh no!' Wendy wailed. 'I only wanted to give them a nice surprise, and now look what's happened!'

Luckily no-one was hurt, but the bus driver was furious.

41

'Look at my beautiful new bus!' He shook his fist at Wendy. She flew off hastily.

Round the corner outside the bank was a big white van. The driver was looking worried because he couldn't make the engine start.

'Here's my chance to do some nice magic at last!' thought Wendy Witch. She looked in the window. In the back she could see a second man with a lady and a little girl.

She told the driver, 'Don't worry! I'll make your engine start.'

And she said:

'You will have no further trouble
Engine start up, at the double!'

And the engine roared into life. The driver set off at once without saying thank-you.

'That's strange! What a rude man,' Wendy said. 'Never mind, I've done some nice magic after all.' And Wendy beamed with happiness.

But not for long. Out of the bank ran a very cross bank manager, with his hands tied behind his back.

'You stupid witch! You've let those robbers escape!' he roared. His face was red with fury.

'They took two hostages – a lady and her daughter, who happened to be in the bank – as well as fifty thousand pounds!'

Wendy felt awful. 'What a mess I'm making of doing nice magic!' she moaned. 'What *can* I do to put things right? Come on, Midnight, we'd better follow the van and try to stop the robbers.'

So off they flew on the broomstick, high in the air this time, so that Wendy soon spotted the van in the distance. The faster it drove, the faster Wendy flew.

The robbers raced out of town on the motorway

'Faster, broomstick!' Wendy urged, and it went as fast as the wind. Wendy's hair streamed out behind her, and Midnight clung on to Wendy's shoulder by her claws. Soon they had caught up with the van. It drove off the motorway onto an old aerodrome that nobody used any more. Waiting there, was a small aeroplane.

The robbers jumped out of the van and ran to the plane, pulling the lady and child with them. Then they came back for the sacks of money. One of the robbers, who was a pilot, started the plane's engines.

Up above, the broomstick flew in circles.

endy was in a flap. 'They're going to take off! We could *never* keep up with an aeroplane! What on earth shall I do?'

As the plane began to move, Midnight miaowed. Wendy remembered that a witch's cat can turn into any creature she wishes. 'Right, Midnight, it's time to earn your keep,' she said. 'It's bad magic time again. Here goes!'

Wendy landed in front of the plane and said:

'As any creature you can be,
Become an elephant for me!'

The robbers in the plane were amazed to see a huge elephant blocking the runway. The pilot slammed on his brakes.

'You can't take off with an elephant on the runway!' yelled Wendy gleefully. But the plane turned round and began to gather speed in the other direction. Wendy thought hard. And she said,

'You won't get off the ground today
Because my eagle's in the way!'

In a flash, the elephant turned into a great bird which swooped in front of the pilot's window. He couldn't see past the bird, so he had to swerve. When he turned the plane the other way and tried to go fast enough to take off, there was the witch on her broomstick flying straight at him. He turned again.

The plane went round and round in circles. 'I'm getting dizzy!' moaned the pilot.

'Pull yourself together,' the other robber told him. 'We must get away before the police arrive.'

Then his mouth fell open in surprise. There was a dinosaur on the runway! The pilot turned the plane – only to find a tall giraffe

looking down at him. Wherever they turned there seemed to be some new animal.

'It can't be!' The pilot rubbed his eyes. 'How did a WHALE get on the runway?'

By the time that the police got there, the plane had stopped. Inside they found two dizzy and frightened robbers. Both of them were tightly wrapped up in the coils of a very long snake. The policemen handcuffed the men and thanked Wendy for catching the robbers.

'You did very well, Miss,' said the sergeant. 'I expect the bank manager will have a reward for you. By the way, where did you get that snake?'

'What snake?' said Wendy. And when the sergeant looked, the snake had disappeared. There was only a small black cat purring on Wendy's shoulder.

The police inspector came up with another man, who hugged the lady and the little girl who had been hostages. Wendy saw it was the bus driver.

'I'm sorry I was cross with you this morning,' he said to Wendy. 'Thank you for rescuing my wife and daughter.' And he gave Wendy a big kiss.

Back at home that night, Wendy gave

Midnight an extra large bowl of milk.

'You did very well today,' she told her. 'But I think that the wizards were right. Bad magic is a lot more fun!'

5 · Witchcraft while you wait

Midnight jumped up on the bed where
Wendy Witch lay peacefully asleep. She sat
on the pillow, said 'Miaow,' and patted
Wendy on the nose with her paw.

Wendy opened one eye. Then up she leapt,
scattering bedclothes everywhere.

'Midnight!' she shrieked. 'What on earth is
the time? We've got to open the new shop!
Hurry up, or we'll be late!'

Before you could say 'abracadabra' Wendy
was dressed in her long gown and pointed hat.
Munching a tasty sandwich of bats' wings and
spiders' webs, she flew out of the house and
tore off down the road.

Wendy Witch had bought a little shop in
the High Street with the reward money she
was given for catching the bank robbers. She
had decided to do some spells for other people.

The sign above the shop read: **'W. Witch
and Cat Ltd: Magic Spells.'** *Spells to Order*
proclaimed a large red poster, and a blue one

announced, *Witchcraft While You Wait*.

Wendy put up more notices reading *Bewitching Bargains* and *Sizzling Savings on Sorcery*.

'It's much too bright and clean in here for a witchcraft shop,' thought Wendy. So she rubbed a bit more dust on the windows, and put up some more cobwebs. Then she switched off all the lights and lit a few candles instead.

'It looks nice and dark and gloomy!' said Wendy, pleased with herself. 'Now for some bats!'

She opened a box and out came several bats, which flew off to the darkest corners to hang upside down from the ceiling. Midnight tried to jump high enough to catch one but couldn't manage it, and went to sleep on the counter instead, next to the sign which said, **Nice** *magic only*.

'It's no time for sleeping, Midnight!' said Wendy Witch. 'Everything is just right, and it's time for the Grand Opening!'

She threw open the door proudly. 'I expect there'll be a queue of customers waiting.'

In came a man in a suit.

'Can I help you, sir?' asked Wendy eagerly.

'Yes, please can you tell me the way to the railway station?'

Wendy told him.

In came the woman from the ladies' hats shop next door. She looked round suspiciously.

'Funny sort of shop you've got here,' she said. 'I wouldn't be surprised if it frightened all my customers away. You'll give the High Street a bad name!' She sniffed indignantly and stalked off.

'I wouldn't mind putting a bad spell on her,' glowered Wendy.

A little boy came in and looked around with interest. But soon his face fell.

'Got no Space Invader machines?' he said. 'Rotten shop!'

And off he went too.

'What a terrible morning!' wailed Wendy. 'Surely *somebody* wants a magic spell done!' Midnight only purred in reply, as she had fallen asleep again.

'Can you really do magic spells?' said a voice, making Wendy jump.

A man stood in the doorway.

'I want you to put a spell on my next door neighbours' children. They scream and shout at all hours of the day and night. I get no peace. Something quite simple would do – turn them into frogs perhaps, or make them

all disappear to the North Pole.'

'No, no, I couldn't do anything like that!' Wendy said, very shocked. 'I only do nice spells in the shop.' She pointed to the sign on the counter.

'Funny sort of witch you are, then!' he said. 'Isn't there anything you could do? Turn them to stone? Make their house burn down?'

'I won't do that,' Wendy told him. 'But I have an idea. Give me your name and address and I might be able to help you.'

'I'm Henry Dickenson,' said the man, and gave Wendy his address. 'I hope you'll think of something,' he said, and left the shop. Then his head popped back round the door again. 'Something with boiling oil in it?' he asked hopefully.

'Certainly not!' laughed Wendy, and gave Midnight a delighted squeeze. 'Our first real customer at last!'

Wendy ate her lunch quickly – deadly nightshade salad, one of her favourites – and she had hardly finished when a girl with red hair in bunches walked in. Her freckled face looked very unhappy.

'Is this the place for magic spells?' she asked. She took Wendy's hand.

'Please put a spell on my horrible brother! He pulls my hair, he pinches my comics, he puts his white mice in my bed. And he's so lazy he won't do any washing up.'

52

'What would you like me to do?' Wendy asked.

'I want you to give him a nasty shock to make him pull his socks up! Make his nose grow long whenever he pinches my sweets; or make his chair grow prickles whenever he sits down instead of washing up.'

'I don't think I could do that,' frowned Wendy. 'You see, I only do nice spells.' She pointed to the sign on the counter. 'But I might be able to help you if you give me your name and address.'

'Oh, thank you!' said the girl. 'I'm Mandy.' She gave Wendy her address.

When Mandy had gone, Wendy did a happy dance around the shop. 'That's two customers already, Midnight!'

Midnight mewed doubtfully as if to say, 'That's all very well, Wendy, but you haven't done any magic spells yet!'

Soon a boy walked in. He, too, had red hair and freckles and was sucking a lollipop. 'Look here!' he said to Wendy. 'Can you do anything about my sister? She nags me all the time! Do this, do that, stop this, stop that; she goes on and on and I get no peace! She's always telling me off! How much for a spell to strike her dumb? My ears need a rest!'

'I can't do that,' said Wendy, and she explained about the sign on the counter. 'But give me your name and address and I think I can help you.' So he did, and Wendy closed the shop as it was time for tea.

After her tea of crunchy dragon's scales and chips, Wendy set to work mixing powders and potions from the different coloured jars on the shelves behind the counter.

'Where's my new cauldron? Ah yes, under the counter. Now, first a pint of Pink Powder, next a gross of Green Grains; now a crowd of Cream Crystals, and stir, and stir – no, Midnight, don't fall in, terrible things could happen to you.'

And Wendy mixed and stirred and mumbled a magic spell, then flew home and slept soundly, happy to have done a good day's work.

Next day, the first in the shop was young Mandy.

'Thank you so much for the wonderful spell! My brother has been so nice since last night – he even shared his sweets with me. I can hardly stop him being kind and helpful.'

Mandy paid for the spell out of her pocket money and left happily.

Later, in came the freckle-faced boy, whose sister nagged him.

'How much do you want for your spell – it worked marvellously! My sister has stopped nagging ever since last night! Here's the money – it was worth every penny!' And he left, whistling happily.

The next to call was Henry Dickenson.

'Let me pay you for the magic spell – it worked wonders. My neighbours' children have been quiet since last night. Did you turn them into frogs after all?'

'Of course not,' smiled Wendy.

'How did you manage it then?'

'Well, after you were here yesterday a girl called Mandy came in and when I saw her address I realised that she lived next door to you. She wanted her brother to stop being so horrible to her, so I expect that's what the arguing and shouting you heard was about.

Then, in came a boy who turned out to be Mandy's brother. He wanted me to stop his sister nagging him. So I put a spell on him to make him kinder. He started being nice to his sister; she started being nice to him because she had nothing to nag him about any more; so they had no rows to disturb your peace. Simple!'

'Well done!' said Henry Dickenson. 'I shall tell all my friends about your shop. I expect you'll have lots of customers from now on!'

And she did.

6 · The battle of Crabley-on-Sea

Wendy Witch was in her Magic Spells Shop one sunny morning. There were no customers in the shop, so she was straightening a few cobwebs, dusting some of the bats, and tidying the jars and bottles of magic powder whose bright colours filled the shelves behind the counter.

'As it's so quiet,' Wendy decided, 'I think I'll take a trip down the High Street to look at the shops.'

A cupboard burst open and Wendy's broomstick shot eagerly out, excited at the prospect of an outing.

'Keep calm, broomstick!' said Wendy sternly, 'we're only going along the street.'

The broomstick had been getting a bit up-pity recently, ever since Wendy had given it a voice so it could remind her when to fill it up with petrol. It didn't have much to say; mostly it grumbled.

Wendy closed the shop and flew along the

pavement, being careful not to knock anybody over. She looked in the baker's at some tempting cakes, then in some clothes shops. Passing the Job Centre, something caught her eye. Flying back, she looked at a small card in the window.

WITCH WANTED
Urgent job for qualified Witch
Crabley-on-Sea 42731.

'It *is* a job for a witch!' said Wendy excitedly. 'And at the sea-side too! That might be lovely in this sunny weather. What do you think, broomstick?'

The broomstick was very keen on the idea, and could hardly keep still while Wendy copied down the telephone number. Then they flew off to find a telephone box.

It was hard to squeeze into the box, particularly as the broomstick would keep wriggling. But finally Wendy got the number dialled. A lady's voice answered.

'The Mayoress of Crabley,' it said. Wendy explained about the job.

'Oh yes!' the Lady Mayoress said. 'We're in such a mess here. Malicious the Magician is spoiling everything for the holidaymakers. Yesterday he made it snow – in midsummer!

58

Can you come at once, before all our tourists go home?'

'Why not?' thought Wendy. 'I'll be on the afternoon flight,' she told the Lady Mayoress.

'Did you hear that, broomstick? We're off to the seaside!' But the broomstick had got out of the telephone box already and was leaning against it, not realising he was jamming the door closed.

At last, after a lot of banging on the windows, Wendy got out, flew home, changed into her best witch's gown, picked up Midnight the cat, and set off for Crabley-on-Sea; not forgetting to fill the broomstick up with petrol before they left.

'What's this for?' said the broomstick. 'I thought we were going by plane!'

'Whatever made you think that?' replied Wendy. 'The afternoon flight is you!'

The broomstick cheered up considerably, and put on its best speed over the hills, cities, towns, valleys, and villages towards the sea.

When they arrived at Crabley, all seemed well. The sun was hot and the beaches full of sunbathers. Children splashed and swam happily in the shallow sea water. There was no sign of Malicious the Magician.

'Looks like a dry spell,' said Wendy, sitting

on the warm sand, wondering whether to change into her bikini. A voice said:

'That's what you think! Here comes a wet spell!' And a cackle of cruel laughter made Wendy and the other sunbathers turn towards a windbreak.

From behind the windbreak appeared Malicious the Magician, chuckling with evil glee. He waved his magic wand and said:

> *'To spoil your fun is what I've planned,*
> *I'll turn to mud this golden sand!'*

There were shrieks from people on the beach as they felt the slithery wet mud on their backs. Children cried when their sand-castles and towers sagged into shapeless muddy heaps. Some people's deckchairs even started to slither and slide slowly towards the sea!

Wendy Witch tried to get up but slipped into the nasty sticky mud until her best gown was covered with it!

Finally she got to her feet and tried to think of a spell to put the mess right again. And she said sadly,

> *'Come back and have a lovely time!*
> *Let sand return, and go away, slime!'*

But the damage had been done, for many

of the holidaymakers had already left in their cars, fed up with Crabley-on-Sea.

Wendy could see the Lady Mayoress on the promenade, upset because the people were leaving. Wendy felt sorry for her.

'You haven't been much help so far, have you?' said the broomstick.

'Oh, shut up!' Wendy answered crossly. 'Now let me think, broomstick. I've got to stop Malicious the Magician somehow.'

The next morning Wendy got up early and was down at the beach in a trice, with Midnight hanging on to the hem of her gown for fear of being left behind. As they settled on the sand, she said, 'This is my plan, broomstick. I'm going to put a good spell on the beach to protect it from any of Malicious the Magician's evil magic!'

Wendy beamed with delight at the cleverness of her idea.

'Don't suppose it'll work,' grumbled the broomstick, annoyed at having to get up so early.

'Nonsense, broomstick, it's a fine idea. Don't you think so, Midnight?' The cat purred her agreement. And Wendy said,

> *'Come down to Crabley beach today,*
> *No harm shall come to you, I say!'*

And she scattered some magic powder all over the beach.

'That should do it!' thought Wendy happily, and settled down to enjoy the sun.

Soon the holidaymakers came back to enjoy the good weather, too. Then Wendy saw Malicious at the other end of the beach. He was waving his wand and looking very cross. His spells wouldn't work – Wendy's magic was too strong!

But suddenly, Wendy, who was getting quite brown, began to feel a little cold. A cloud had covered the sun.

'That's funny, Midnight. The sky was clear a minute ago.' Then she saw Malicious the Magician on a tall rock. He was summoning up the clouds.

'Oh no!' moaned Wendy. 'I put my magic on the beach but forgot the sky!'

Malicious waved his wand and larger and darker clouds appeared. Then came lightning, thunder, rain, and even hailstones. Not a raindrop touched the beach, protected by Wendy Witch's spell, but above, the storm raged.

The people began to leave the beach. It was no fun sunbathing beneath a storm!

'Perhaps I could chase him off,' Wendy

thought. She noticed a crab near her on a rock and it gave her an idea. She said:

> *'All the crabs on Crabley Beach,*
> *Chase Malicious out of reach!'*

Many huge crabs began to gather. They had big pincers that could give you a nasty nip. They set off towards the magician's rock.

Other crabs from the rocks, the pools, even from under the wet sand at the water's edge, came to join the march. There were brown and green ones, smooth and hairy ones, large ones and now a lot of small ones too.

Wendy was so interested in watching the crabs that she didn't see Malicious waving his wand at them.

The next thing she knew, the army of crabs had turned on *her*.

The first crab sunk its pincers into her toe. In no time, two more scuttled right up on her shoulders, then more arrived to cling on to her gown.

'Ooh! Ouch!' yelled Wendy, and rushed off the beach with Midnight and the broomstick, trying to shake off the crabs as she went.

Many nips and pinches later, she reached the safety of the promenade, out of breath, her pointed hat askew.

'His magic wand is as strong as my spells,' she panted. 'I'll never win as long as he has that wand.' And Wendy flew dejectedly back to the hotel.

The next morning, Wendy flew up and down the beach, with Midnight on her shoulder, alert for the first sign of the magician.

'Now listen!' she told the broomstick. 'I've worked out another plan. This is what *you* have to do.'

'Me?' The broomstick sounded doubtful. 'It's got nothing to do with crabs, has it?' It looked round warily.

Wendy explained the broomstick's job. Then the sight of some seagulls gave her another idea. She said to them:

> *'When you see the Wizard, do this for me:*
> *Snatch his wand, and throw it in the sea!'*

A little group of five grey and white gulls bobbed up and down on the sea and looked as if they quite understood what Wendy wanted.

The beach was not very full, as many people had left Crabley-on-Sea, but still a few children splashed happily in the surf around a wooden raft in the bay.

Suddenly Malicious the Magician appeared on the raft. He waved his wand about him, whipping the sea into high columns and pillars of foam. The children were in danger!

'Right!' called Wendy. 'Off you go, broomstick!' It set off at speed towards the magician. The seagulls, too, took to the air. Then she said:

'Little cat, so small and dark,
Turn at once into a shark!'

And she tossed Midnight towards the waves.

Then the wicked magician conjured up a huge wave. It raced towards the beach getting bigger and bigger. It curled over and broke on to the sand just where Wendy Witch was standing. She vanished under the mountain of water.

Malicious cackled with delight, but not for long. The seagulls had swooped down from the sky and snatched his magic wand. Then they flew far out to sea and dropped it. Malicious stamped his foot with rage – his wand was lost for ever!

Then the broomstick shot straight between the magician's ankles as he stood on the raft. It twisted and tripped him over into the sea! Without his wand he was helpless to make any more spells and now, the menacing black fin of a shark swam circles around him!

Wendy was left drenched, bedraggled, and covered in seaweed from the giant wave but she didn't care – her plan had worked!

'Help!' called Malicious the Magician. 'Save me! I can't swim! That's why I've been spoiling everyone's fun! I hate to see them enjoying themselves when I can't swim!'

'If I save you,' Wendy answered sternly from the shore, 'you must promise never to cause trouble in Crabley-on-Sea again.'

'Very well, I promise. Please get me out. You've won!'

So Wendy allowed the broomstick to haul the wet and miserable magician to the beach.

'Well done, Wendy!' said the Lady Mayoress. 'Now people can

enjoy their holidays in peace!'

Wendy Witch decided to stay for a few days' holiday at Crabley-on-Sea. The next morning she could be seen in the swimming pool. There, too, was Malicious the Magician – with armbands on. Wendy was teaching him to swim!

7 · The broomstick goes on strike

One morning, while Wendy Witch was putting up some extra cobwebs in her Magic Spells shop, the bell jangled and the headmaster of Hilltop School came in. Mr. Williams usually had a kindly smile and a twinkle in his eye, but today he looked worried.

'Ah, Wendy,' he said. 'Some strange things have been happening at my school. Very strange indeed. In fact, I think it may be a job for a witch. Will you come to the school and help me?'

'I'll come as soon as I've closed the shop,' promised Wendy and Mr. Williams left the shop saying, 'It's puzzling! Very puzzling indeed!' and scratching his grey head.

'Come on, broomstick! called Wendy. 'This sounds like an exciting new job for us.'

She expected the broomstick to come bursting eagerly out of its cupboard as it usually did. But today, instead, it trailed out in a sulk.

Wendy didn't notice, as she had just

realised that the floor of the shop was in a terrible mess.

'Oh, broomstick, give the floor a sweep before we go,' she said. 'It's in an awful state.'

But the broomstick paid no attention.

'Why should I have to do all the dirty jobs while you do all the important magic?' it sulked. 'It's not fair! I'm going on strike!'

'On strike? But how shall I get to the school without a broomstick?'

'You've got legs, haven't you?' the broomstick answered rudely. 'You'll just have to walk!'

'But how can I be a *proper* witch without a broomstick?' wailed Wendy.

It was no good. The broomstick flounced back into its cupboard and slammed the door. Wendy couldn't persuade it to come out again.

'We shall just have to walk then, Midnight,' she said, giving the cat a hug. 'At least *you're* not on strike.' So they set off for the school, Wendy feeling very sorry for herself.

When they got to Hilltop School, Wendy went straight to Mr. Williams' office.

'Ah, Wendy, I'm glad you've come! Let me show you round the school and you'll see the strange things I told you about.'

Just then Midnight miaowed. It was more of a yowl than a miaow. Wendy turned to see her cat by the fireplace. Midnight's back was arched and her hair stood on end. She seemed very upset. Wendy whisked her up and carried her out of the office.

'Don't you start, Midnight! I've got enough trouble with the broomstick misbehaving.'

In the first classroom Wendy saw a cross teacher trying to write on the blackboard. But her chalk wouldn't write. Some children were trying to sharpen pencils, but however hard they tried the pencils still came out blunt.

'It's the same all over the school,' Mr. Williams told Wendy, 'Nothing works!'

In the next room a record spun merrily on the turntable of a record player, but no music played!

They called in at the kitchens. The cook, a large red-faced lady, was waving a ladle.

'Mr. Williams! I have been cooking this meat in hot ovens for two hours, but it's *still* raw! How can I be expected to provide dinner under these conditions?' She waved a slice of raw beef under the nose of the headmaster. The kitchen ladies scuttled nervously about their work, trying to keep out of the way of the ladle.

Wendy and Mr. Williams hastily left the kitchens and visited another classroom.

'Oh no! It's even worse than I thought!' Mr. Williams exclaimed. 'The children have all gone to sleep!'

Not only were the children fast asleep, but the teacher, too, was slumped at her desk. Mr. Williams gave her shoulders a shake. She stirred and mumbled, 'Seven sixes are . . .' and a voice at the back of the class answered sleepily, 'Thirty-five, Miss . . .' before both settled down to sleep again, the teacher quietly snoring.

'Now you can see the problem, Wendy. Can you do anything to help?' begged Mr. Williams.

'What? Oh!' said Wendy. She was still puzzling over whether thirty-five was the right

answer to the sum. 'Now let me think.' Then
she said:

> *'Give Mr. Williams no more strife*
> *Everything come back to life!'*

Mr. Williams was delighted to see the
teacher and the children begin to wake up.
But then things started to go terribly wrong.
The spell had worked – but not the way
Wendy had expected!

The tables and chairs came back to life. As
they were made of wood, they began to turn
back into trees, and grew branches and leaves!

In the next classroom, the pencil sharpener
had started to work on its own! It flew about
the room finding pencils to sharpen, then
sharpened them right down to the end till
there was none left. The chalk, too, had
started to work on its own and was busily
writing nonsense on the blackboard all by
itself.

'Oh dear!' Wendy wailed. 'This wasn't
what I meant at all!'

In the music room the record player was
working on its own, even though the teacher
had unplugged it! It spun round far too fast
so that the music sounded all squeaky.

There was worse to come. Suddenly the

dining room doors burst open and the kitchen ladies ran out shrieking. Right behind them lumbered three large cows. Even the beef had come back to life!

The angry cook marched up to the headmaster, still waving her ladle dangerously.

'Mr. Williams, this is too much! I'm leaving right now!'

'I'm so sorry, Mr. Williams,' said Wendy miserably. 'My spell went all wrong.'

'Never mind,' said the headmaster kindly. 'I'm sure you did the best you could.'

On the way out, a lawn mower which had begun to work on its own chased Wendy and Midnight to the gate.

Wendy ran all the way back to the shop.

'I'll just have to ask the Blue Witch what to do,' she decided.

She now had to wait till twelve o'clock midnight when she knew the Blue Witch would fly past her chimney, so she went to open the broomstick's cupboard to see if it would fly her home.

'I've had a terrible day, broomstick,' she pleaded. 'Won't you please fly me home?'

'Absolutely not,' insisted the broomstick. 'Haven't you seen my banners?'

Wendy looked. Around its cupboard the

broomstick had stuck posters which read, 'More Important Work for Broomsticks' and 'Dirty Jobs Strike.'

'What happened that was so terrible, anyway?' asked the broomstick, who was very curious, even though it was on strike.

'My magic spell went wrong!' wailed Wendy. 'Everything that was made of wood turned into trees, and grew leaves ... just a minute, that gives me an idea! Come on, Midnight.'

A wicked gleam came into Wendy's eye. She picked up the broomstick and put it over one shoulder, Midnight perched on the other, and she marched home. The broomstick grumbled about being treated in this undignified manner.

'Well, you won't carry me, so I shall have to carry you,' Wendy replied in her firmest voice.

When they got home, Wendy took the broomstick into the garden. She turned it upside-down and planted it in the soil. 'Ow!' it protested. 'What are you up to now?'

'This will teach you to be a nuisance!' laughed Wendy gleefully, and said:

> *'Give a poor witch no more strife*
> *All your sticks come back to life!'*

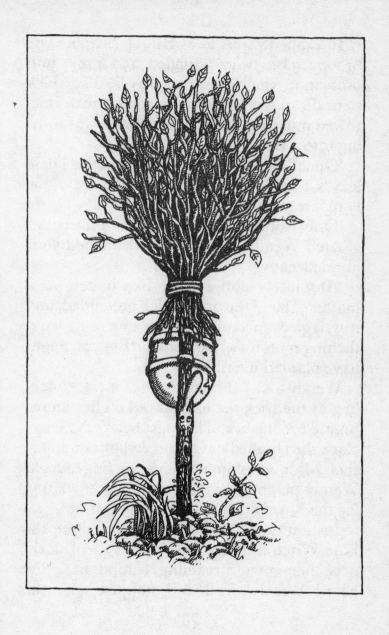

It happened just as at Hilltop School. The broomstick's twigs wriggled and grew into branches, which sprouted leaves. The thick stem down the centre grew roots which burrowed into the soil. The broomstick was turning into a tree.

'Ouch!' protested the broomstick. 'These leaves tickle! You aren't going to leave me here, are you?'

'Only for as long as you're on strike,' gloated Wendy. 'Or have you changed your mind already?'

'Absolutely not! I quite like it here as a matter of fact,' the broomstick pretended, and it wriggled uncomfortably as one of its lengthening roots hit a sharp stone. 'But you might have planted me right way up!'

Wendy took Midnight inside for tea, chuckling at the trick she had played on her unfortunate broomstick. Then just before twelve o' clock she climbed out of the skylight on to the roof. Midnight skipped along the ridge tiles as Wendy perched by the chimney pot, waiting for the Blue Witch to fly by.

Just on the witching hour of midnight, the Blue Witch appeared out of the silent darkness, her gown streaming behind her. She heard Wendy's call and stopped near the chimney. The wise old witch listened to Wendy's tale of the strange happenings at Hilltop School.

'I have heard,' the old witch croaked, 'that a skeleton lies hidden in that school and that, until it is found and buried, the school will be haunted by troubles and misfortunes. Find the skeleton, Wendy, and your problem will be solved.' And off she flew.

Wendy frowned and puzzled over the Blue Witch's words. Then Midnight sprang on to the chimney beside her, and suddenly Wendy's face lit up in a beam of delight.

'Oh, thank you, Midnight! You've just reminded me. Now I know what to do!'

Happily she waved after the old witch, till she could no longer be seen.

The next morning Wendy leapt out of bed at first light.

'Come on, Midnight, we must get to the school early today – there's work to be done!'

They waved cheerfully to the broomstick before setting off. It was looking sorry for itself, and trying to shake the last night's dew off its damp leaves.

Wendy ran all the way to Hilltop School and arrived quite out of breath. No-one was there but Mr. Williams, who was quite alarmed to see her so excited. Then he found her a torch, though he couldn't imagine why she wanted it.

Wendy went straight to the fireplace and peered up the chimney. Sure enough, high up inside the old chimney, she could see some bones.

'The Blue Witch told me there was a skeleton in the school,' she said breathlessly, 'but it was Midnight who gave me the clue where to look by behaving so strangely at this fireplace yesterday.' And she explained to the amazed headmaster about the haunting of Hilltop School.

'But how are we going to get the skeleton out?' Wendy puzzled.

'How about your broomstick? It could fly up the chimney and sweep it out,' Mr. Williams suggested.

Wendy rushed home again. 'My feet are worn out!' she wailed 'and all because of that obstinate broomstick!'

'How are you feeling, broomstick?' she asked when they reached the garden.

'Rooted to the spot,' it said in surly tones.

'It's a pity you're on strike,' Wendy went on. 'You could have had the chance to stop the haunting of Hilltop School all by yourself.

You would have been a hero.'

'A hero? You mean, a really important job?'

'Oh yes! The most important one of all.'

'Oh, well, that's different,' the broomstick said. 'Get me out of this mess and I'll do it.'

Wendy joyfully said:

> *'Broomstick, you've been in a scrape*
> *But come back now to normal shape!'*

And soon they were soaring and swooping happily back to Hilltop School.

The broomstick went to work up the chimney. The children waiting in the playground heard a rustling and a scraping. Then out popped the proud broomstick from the chimney, with the skeleton sitting astride it. The children cheered.

'I've arranged for the skeleton to go to a local museum,' a smiling Mr. Williams told Wendy. 'Thank you for all you have done.'

Wendy turned and picked up Midnight. 'Thank heavens we can fly home now, Midnight. I've done enough walking to last a month!'

But the heroic broomstick was far too busy

to give them a lift home. It was giving rides to the admiring children in the playground.

So Wendy and Midnight had to walk home – again!

8 · Vanishing land

'Soon we can be invisible whenever we want to, Midnight!'

Wendy Witch was excited. The Green Wizard was coming to her shop and he had promised to show her how to make his vanishing powder.

Midnight didn't seem impressed, but went on happily chasing a ball of string round the floor.

Wendy took out her cauldron ready to mix the ingredients and lit some candles in the shop. 'I hope he'll come,' she said anxiously. 'It's raining harder than ever.'

She needn't have worried. The Green Wizard's broomstick came swooping down out of a dark sky.

'Bad Morning, Wendy!' said the Green Wizard, squelching soggily into the shop. He wrung out his wet beard on to the mat and hung up his umbrella on the end of Wendy's broomstick behind the door.

The broomstick thought about protesting, but saw Wendy's warning look and decided not to. Although it was now a hero, the broomstick was much more obedient since the time that Wendy changed it into a tree.

'There you are – all the ingredients for vanishing powder!' The Green Wizard proudly showed Wendy the many pockets inside his cape. Every one had a jar or box or packet or bottle inside it.

Wendy watched excitedly as he took them out and placed them carefully on the counter one by one. They were all different colours.

'It's taken a lifetime to collect them all! But you must remember,' he warned her sternly, 'that vanishing powder is very tricky stuff. If you don't mix it just right, or if you swallow too much or too little, things can go wrong.'

'What do you mean?' Wendy asked.

'Well, if the mixture's wrong, you could vanish when you don't want to instead of when you do. Or, if you take too little, only bits of you could disappear instead of all of you.'

'What if you get it just right?'

'Well, then you become invisible, and though you are there all the time, nobody can see you.'

'What if you swallow too much?' asked Wendy, thrilled.

'Ah well, then you really do disappear altogether, to Vanishing Land, and nobody knows when you'll get back.'

Wendy was horrified. 'Have you ever been there?'

'Oh yes,' the Wizard said thoughtfully, 'but I don't want to talk about it. Now, shall we start the mixing?'

Each ingredient had to be carefully weighed on the scales before it went in the cauldron. Midnight was fascinated by the rocking of the scales as they weighed out the powder. She jumped on the counter to get a good view. She put her paw on one pan of the scales to make it rock. Twice Wendy had to weigh some crystals again because Midnight upset the scales.

At last Wendy got cross. 'Midnight, you nuisance, go away!' she scolded, and waved her hand at the cat. 'Or we'll get nothing done today!'

Just then the shop door banged open and a gust of wind blew out all the candles. Wendy and the Green Wizard were suddenly in the dark! Wendy rushed to bolt the door and Midnight took the chance she had been waiting for. She leapt into the cauldron to have a lick at the tasty looking mixture. She hoped it was something new and exciting for supper.

But what a disappointment! It tasted rather bitter. So Midnight lost interest, climbed out, and jumped down behind the counter. Then she padded softly down the corridor to the little room behind the shop.

But she never got there. Half way through the door the magic powder worked and Midnight disappeared to Vanishing Land.

It was a while before Wendy could find her matches and light all the candles again. By that time Midnight was nowhere to be seen.

'Thank heavens for that!' said Wendy with relief. 'Now we can get on with our work. What's next?'

'The mixture's nearly ready!' the Green Wizard told her. 'Just a touch of Purple Powder, now ... pass that packet by your elbow, Wendy.' And they bent over the cauldron again.

'There!' beamed the Green Wizard at last. 'The vanishing powder is just right!' He gave the mixture one last stir. 'You can try it right now if you want, Wendy.'

But Wendy was rather worried that Midnight hadn't come back. It was long past her feeding time. She had never missed *that* before!

She gave the Green Wizard a quick hug for all his hard work, but told him: 'It wouldn't feel right to start vanishing without Midnight. I'm so used to having her with me, you see, when I do my magic. I'll just see if I can find her.'

The rain had stopped at last. Wendy flew up and down the streets. She searched the back alleys. She made the broomstick take her all round the park, and then down to the shopping precinct. There was no sign of her cat.

Wendy met the lollipop lady, but she hadn't seen Midnight. Nor had Mr. Price, who was just closing his shop. She asked P.C. Trunch, but he couldn't help either.

The broomstick was getting fed up. 'Why all this fuss about a cat?' it grumbled.

'Midnight has helped me in all my adventures,' Wendy retorted. 'Remember when she stopped the bank robbers escaping? And when she saved Jimmy's ice-cream van that was going to crash? I miss my little cat!' And a tear ran down Wendy Witch's cheek. 'I wish I hadn't told her to go away!' she wailed.

Wendy flew sadly back to the shop.

'I can't find Midnight anywhere!' she moaned.

'I've been thinking,' said the Green Wizard. 'What did you say exactly, when you told your cat to go away?'

Wendy thought. 'I remember now. I said:

Midnight, you nuisance, go away!
Or we'll get nothing done today!'

'That's right!' said the wizard. You said it in rhyme, so –'

'It worked like a spell –' said Wendy.

'– and the stormy weather made sure it was a good strong spell!'

'Well, if a spell made her disappear, a spell can bring her back,' said Wendy firmly. She tried hard to think of the right spell. Then she said:

'Wherever in the town you may be,
Come here, black cat, come here to me.'

Instantly, Wendy was at the centre of a wriggling mass of black fur. All the black cats in town were in Wendy's shop in a struggling heap. Soon they were scratching and screeching, howling and spitting at each other.

And not one of them was Midnight.

Wendy Witch was exhausted by the time she had chased all the cats out of the shop. She went to see if any cats had got into the back room. That was when she found Midnight's paw prints.

'They must be Midnight's,' she said. 'The other cats didn't come this way.'

89

The Green Wizard looked closely at the paw prints.

'This is vanishing powder!' he exclaimed. 'Midnight must have got in the cauldron when the wind blew the candles out. Look! The tracks come to an end in the doorway. I'm afraid your cat has swallowed some powder. She must be in Vanishing Land, or she would have come back by now.'

'In Vanishing Land! Oh no! My poor little cat!' Wendy wailed. 'Now I might never get her back. I wish you'd never brought that awful powder!'

Wendy was so upset and cross, she blamed it all on the Green Wizard.

'I've lost poor Midnight, small and black –
I wish your beard grew down the back!'

The surprised wizard felt his chin. It was bare! But the long, straggly beard wasn't growing down his back either. They soon found it – growing down *Wendy's* back!

Meanwhile, Midnight strolled along pleasant paths in Vanishing Land. She came to a valley full of all the things that conjurers had made vanish on the stage. There were rabbits, and doves; there were playing cards, and coins; all these had ended up in Vanishing

Land. There were magicians' assistants, whose magicians were clever enough to make them disappear, but not clever enough to get them back. They were delighted to see Midnight, so they played with her and petted her. Midnight purred with contentment.

Then she found a garden full of all those things that people lose. Every time a boy getting ready for school says, 'Mum! My tie's vanished again!' or his sister shrieks, 'Where's my other glove?' or his dad grumbles, 'Now where have my keys got to this time?' or his mum complains, 'Who's had my pen? I left it right here!' – in fact, every time you lose something and you *know* you left it just there, it's really gone to the Garden of Lost Things in Vanishing Land.

So the little black cat had plenty to play with. There were odd shoes; the last piece of lots of jigsaw puzzles; pairs of glasses, odd socks, buttons; important parts of games and toys; brushes and combs, handkerchiefs, torches, matches, and even the last page of some very exciting books.

Midnight explored happily. Every now and again, something she was playing with would disappear with a pop. And in the real world someone would say: 'My tie's turned up

again!' or 'Oh, look, my glasses were here all
the time!' or 'I told you, your keys were just
where you left them.' And only Midnight
knew differently.

Back in her shop Wendy was sorry as soon
as she put the spell on the Green Wizard's
beard. Of course it wasn't his fault! She
worked some more magic to put his beard
back on his chin.

'You've been so kind,' she moaned. 'What
a terrible way to repay you!'

'Never mind, Wendy, I understand. You

were upset. The main thing is, how are we going to get your cat back? We don't know how much powder she swallowed. If she ate a lot, the magic might not wear off for years.'

'Well, in that case, I must go and fetch her myself,' Wendy decided.

'You mean, go to Vanishing Land? Well, it's risky, but if you're that fond of the cat ...'

'I'd do *anything* to get Midnight back,' said Wendy firmly.

'Then we'll try.' The Green Wizard fiddled with his beard, glad to have it back, then got out the cauldron. 'We don't know the right amount to take, so try just a taste of powder first.'

So Wendy took just a pinch of vanishing powder, and pulled a face at the bitter taste.

'Has it worked yet? Can you see me?' she asked the wizard eagerly.

'You're still there, large as life!' laughed the Green Wizard. 'Go for a walk, and give the magic time to work.'

So Wendy took a stroll in the High Street.

After a while she met P.C. Trunch. She called 'Hello!' to him but the plump policeman suddenly sat down right in the middle of the pavement and rubbed his head.

'Oh no!' he said, 'I'm seeing things! A pair of legs walking down the street on their own? They'll never believe this down at the station!'

Wendy rushed back to the shop to ask the wizard what had happened. The Green Wizard chuckled.

'Well, you're only half gone,' he said, 'but your legs are still there. This time you can have a stronger dose.'

So, when she came back to normal, Wendy tried a larger amount of vanishing powder. Again it didn't work at once, so she took another walk. It was getting dark outside, but the street lights were on.

The bus-driver's wife stopped her husband with a hand on his arm.

'Do you see what I see?'

'It looks like that odd girl who rescued you from the bank robbers,' he answered. 'But I can see right through her! It must be a ghost!'

His wife had already fainted.

Wendy rushed back to the shop. The sight of her gave the Green Wizard a fright.

'Oh, it's you, Wendy,' he said. 'I can see that door right through you. You did give me a turn.'

'This is no good,' Wendy complained. 'I must have more powder.'

So she took a big spoonful, picked up her broomstick, and disappeared.

By now, Midnight was feeling homesick. She'd had a wonderful time in Vanishing Land, but now she just wanted to go home, lap up a saucer of milk, and talk to Wendy about the day's adventures, while the broomstick grumbled as usual.

Suddenly a dark spot appeared against the sky and grew larger. It became a figure with a tall pointed hat riding on a broomstick. It landed and scooped up the delighted cat.

'I've come to take you home, Midnight,' said Wendy, and hugged her cat joyfully. 'What a naughty cat you were, to eat that powder!' Midnight purred happily in Wendy's ear.

'I'm going to hold you tight, Midnight, so when the magic wears off, we'll be sure to go back together. Till then, the broomstick will take us for a ride round Vanishing Land. Won't you, broomstick?'

'I suppose so,' said the Broomstick, 'if we must.'

When they did get back to the real world it was night. They found themselves in headlong flight above the rooftops of the town. Around them Wendy could see dark shapes.

'There's our house,' Wendy cried, as they sped past far above, 'and our Magic Spells Shop.' But they rushed on over the town, towards the distant hills.

Then the moon came out and lit up the mass of dark shapes. Wendy could see they were all witches or wizards on broomsticks, all in swift flight.

'There are dozens of them – hundreds, Midnight! I can see the Blue Witch, and the Grey Wizard. And I think that's the Green Wizard, flying right over there, with his beard streaming behind in the wind. He'll be glad to know I got you back, Midnight.'

Wendy was happy, back with her little cat once more, and her broomstick; it was wonderful to be a witch. Then she remembered what night it was.

'Of course! It's Hallowe'en, Midnight! Tonight the witches fly together. It's time for me to meet them all at last. What a fine time we shall have!'

And they did!